Calvin Coconut

ZOO BREATH

Other Books About Calvin Coconut

Calvin Coconut

ZOO
BREATH

Graham Salisbury

illustrated by
Jacqueline Rogers

WENDY
LAMB
BOOKS

Published by Wendy Lamb Books
an imprint of Random House Children's Books
a division of Random House, Inc.
New York

Wendy Lamb Books and the colophon are trademarks of Random House, Inc.

Visit us on the Web! www.randomhouse.com/kids

Educators and librarians, for a variety of teaching tools, visit us at
www.randomhouse.com/teachers

Library of Congress Cataloging-in-Publication Data
Salisbury, Graham.
Calvin Coconut : zoo breath / Graham Salisbury ;
illustrated by Jacqueline Rogers. — 1st ed.
p.   cm.
Summary: When Calvin gets a school assignment to do some original research,
he decides to investigate his dog's stinky breath and ends up learning
about more than just smells.
ISBN 978-0-385-73704-3 (hc) — ISBN 978-0-385-90642-5 (lib. bdg.) —
ISBN 978-0-375-89739-9 (e-book) [1. Family life—Hawaii—Fiction. 2. Odors—Fiction.
3. Schools—Fiction. 4. Hawaii—Fiction.] I. Rogers, Jacqueline, ill. II. Title.
III. Title: Zoo breath.
PZ7.S15225Cap 2010
[Fic]—dc22
2009040164

Book design by Angela Carlino

Printed in the United States of America

10 9 8 7 6 5 4 3 2 1

First Edition

For
Jake and Duke

Stand tall, always
—G.S.

For Martin
—J.R.

A Good Stink

"**A**ck!" Stella snapped, turning around in the front seat of the car. "Get that thing away from me!"

It was Sunday, and Mom was driving us to the grocery store. Stella was sixteen; she'd come from Texas to live with us and help

Mom. She was in high school, studying ways to mess up my life. Me and my sister, Darci, were in the backseat with Streak, my dog.

Streak was sitting on my knees, hanging her head over the front seat. Breathing on Stella.

I gave Streak a hug and sat back, pulling her close.

She licked my ear.

Stella glared over her shoulder. "Did you just let that stinky dog lick germs all over you?"

"Streak doesn't have germs, and anyway dogs have clean tongues."

Stella shook her head and turned back.

I sniffed the top of Streak's head. "I don't smell any stink."

Stella mumbled, "You wouldn't."

Mom glanced into the rearview mirror. "Stella's right, Calvin. Streak does smell, especially her breath. Maybe she can stick her head out the window instead of hanging over the front seat."

I hugged Streak. So what if she was a little

stinky? All dogs smelled, but it was a good stink, not a bad one. Still, I'd just adopted her from the Humane Society, and 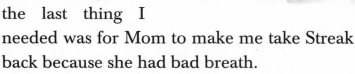 the last thing I needed was for Mom to make me take Streak back because she had bad breath.

I glanced over at Darci, who was bouncing Petey on her knee. Petey was a green, pint-size stuffed parrot with small dried beans in it. Mom's boyfriend, Ledward, had given it to her. Petey was Darci's favorite thing in the world. For now, anyway.

I leaned close and whispered, "Hey, Darce, smell Streak's breath and see if you think it stinks."

Stella had ears like an elephant. "Don't you dare! Don't fall for it, Darci. He's tricking you."

"I am not!" I said.

"Then smell it yourself."

"Pfff," I huffed, then scooted back to my side of the backseat.

I knew Streak's breath was terrible.

Stella smirked. "See, Darci? He won't even do it himself, and it's his dog."

"Will too," I mumbled. But didn't.

I inched Streak forward, aiming her breath at Stella.

"Calvin," Mom said.

Man, she had eyes in the back of her head.

I put the window down and let Streak hang her head out. She loved it. Spit flew off her tongue in the wind.

I was worried.

Really worried.

Because Mom and Stella had been complaining more than usual about Streak: how she smelled, chewed up everything in sight, left dog doo all over the yard, and shed hair in the house—even though she was only allowed in the kitchen to eat. She slept in my room, which wasn't even in the house, but in the garage.

My friend Willy's dog got to be in *his* house.

I slumped in my seat.

Could Mom make me get rid of Streak? Would she?

One time Mom stepped in some of Streak's dog doo in the yard and nearly bit my head off. "I wish you'd gotten a *fish* for a pet!" Then she bought me a shovel and wrote on the handle with a big fat black Sharpie: CALVIN'S POOPER SCOOPER. "Use this every day, rain or shine," she'd said. "Toss the stuff into the bushes, *away* from the house."

Fine. I did that. Rain or shine.

"I can take a lot, Calvin," Mom said now. "But that dog's breath is—"

"Disgusting!" Stella butted in.

I stuck my head out the window with Streak. She was the best dog that ever lived.

But I was going to lose her.

It was just a matter of time.

2

Detectives

Next week in class, Mr. Purdy smiled and spread his hands. "Good morning, boot campers! It's Friday!"

"Good morning, Mr. Purdy," we droned.

I was only half listening because I was thinking about Streak, how she was always so happy to see me when I got home from school.

Mr. Purdy rubbed his hands together. He looked at us, flicked his eyebrows.

Aiy. First the arms, now the eyebrows. This could only mean trouble.

I looked out the window from my front-row seat. Another sunny morning at Kailua Elementary School. Nice day.

To lose a dog.

Stop!

I turned back to Mr. Purdy.

"Okaaay," he said. "Let's get started. Today I'm going to introduce you to something so fun you will think you're on vacation. Ready?"

We all perked up. Vacation?

Shayla bounced in her seat. "What is it, Mr. Purdy?"

Shayla sat next to me. She was a know-it-all pest, and to make things worse, she was always smiling at me. "She thinks you're cute," my friend Maya once told me.

Cute? *Blaaach!*

"Yeah, Mr. Purdy," Rubin shouted from the back. "We going on a class trip or something?"

"That we are, guys, that we are, because today I am going to introduce you to . . . discovery!"

Huh?

"Primary research," Mr. Purdy added.

It got so quiet I could almost hear the ants sneaking up on Shayla's pink-and-purple lunch box.

Doreen raised her hand. "Is that like looking things up and stuff?"

"That would be called secondary research, Doreen, or research that's already been done. This is called *primary* research, which means you'll be the first to do it."

Silence.

Mr. Purdy chuckled. "This will be fun, trust me. You're all going to be detectives. You're going to ask a discovery question, then answer it.

9

You can interview people, make observations, gather and analyze things that haven't been analyzed before. Think of the possibilities!"

This was a vacation?

"Then," Mr. Purdy continued, "you will present your findings to the class. Boy, are we in for a fun time!"

You could have heard a mosquito burp in that classroom.

"Come on, boot campers," Mr. Purdy said. "You've got till next Tuesday. I'm going to show you how fascinating it can be to discover and study something new. And you can study whatever you want. No pressure, no rules, no limits . . . well, I take that back. I wouldn't want you researching the value of picking your nose or why you should sleep in class, of course."

That got a few snickers.

Still, this all sounded like work.

"I urge you to use props, too," Mr. Purdy added.

Rubin raised his hand and spoke at the same time. "What's props, Mr. Purdy?"

"Something to help you present your findings, Rubin. Let's say you discovered something new about cockroaches. Then to help you explain it to the class, you might bring in a cockroach in a container. That would be a prop. You can also make posters, take photographs, or bring in various objects. Those would all be props."

"Cock-a-roaches," I said to myself.

Once, Mr. Purdy made us think of pretzels to start our essays. It was weird. But it worked.

"So," Mr. Purdy said. "What do you want to discover, detectives? What do you want to research that hasn't been researched before? Think about it."

Hmmm.

Maybe I could research something about Las Vegas. Dad had moved there about four years ago with his new wife, Marissa. He was Little Johnny Coconut, the singer. He made up that last name, and then he made it legal. Now it was our for-real last name.

Dad took our dog, Chewy, to Las Vegas when he left.

I smiled, remembering that little rat-nosed mutt. Dad kept him a lot cleaner than I kept Streak. But I figured, why give a dog a bath when she's just going to get dirty all over again?

Hey! An idea for my research project popped into my head.

It was a weird one.

I liked it.

3

Stampede

"How about movies, Mr. Purdy?" Ace asked. "Can we do that?"

"Sure you can. Just come up with a unique question to start things off. Something like 'Why do kids reach under their movie seats to see if someone stuck gum there?' Ask a question, then answer it."

"Ick," Shayla said. "I'm not doing that one."

I grinned, thinking of the question I'd come up with: Why do dogs have stink breath and how can you un-stink it?

Shayla said, "Can we work with a partner, Mr. Purdy?" She glanced at me.

I put my elbows on my desk and covered my face with my hands. Where was that dog breath when you needed it? If Streak had been on my lap I'd have aimed her nose at Shayla. But maybe even that wouldn't make her go away.

"Exactly what I had in mind, Shayla. You will work in teams of two."

Everybody sat up, trying to grab good partners. I glanced at Willy, Julio, and Rubin. Maya, Ace. Anyone but Shayla.

Mr. Purdy showed us a sheet of paper tacked to the bulletin board. "I've already chosen your partners. You may get up—*quietly*—and go see who your fellow detective is."

Chairs screeched back.

Stampeding feet rolled toward the front of the room.

I squeezed my way up to the bulletin board. My partner was–*Julio!*

Yes!

Someone slapped the back of my head and I turned. Julio flicked his eyebrows at me.

I raised a fist and turned back to the list. Who else was paired up?

Willy and Rubin.

Ace and Doreen. I glanced at Ace. How'd he feel about having to work with a girl? He seemed fine with it. He would. He liked everyone, and everyone liked him.

Who else?

Maya and . . . *Shayla?*

Really? They were total opposites.

I turned around to find Maya. This was too funny.

She was sitting at her desk looking like she'd just swallowed a fly.

Mr. Purdy clapped his hands. "All right, find your partners and come up with a research question. You've got ten minutes. Let the discoveries begin!"

"Maya," I said, leaning over her desk. "Did you see who you got?"

She gave me a look that said, Keep talking if you want your eyes scratched out.

I staggered over to Julio's desk, laughing my head off.

4

Stinks

At recess, I sat slumped under a monkeypod tree with Julio, Willy, and Rubin. Maya usually hung out with us, too, but she was hiding. Shayla was looking for her.

I shook my head, grinning. "Can you believe Maya got Shayla?"

"Never work," Julio said. "She'll eat dirt first."

"But she has to be Shayla's partner, right?" Willy said. "I mean, Mr. Purdy—"

Julio humphed. "You don't know Maya. Neither does Mr. Purdy."

"She'll do it," I said. "She won't back down."

Julio stuck out his hand. "Bag of dried shrimp says she doesn't."

"You're on," I said, slapping his palm. "So, partner, got any ideas? Because if you don't, I do."

Rubin wrapped his arm over Willy's shoulder. "Me and Willy got one."

"We do?"

"Yeah, listen. You know how Mr. Purdy said to ask a question? Well, this is it: What's better, Naruto or InuYasha?"

Me and Julio cracked up. "Serious?"

Willy looked confused. "What's Nar . . . what?"

Rubin patted Willy's back. "After school, come my house. I show you."

"They're books," I said. "Manga."

"Manga?"

Julio grinned. "Manga's like comic books. You read um backwards like they do in Japan. Rubin goes there every summer to stay with his grandparents."

Now Willy was really confused. He prob'ly didn't know manga from mangoes.

"Stick with me," Rubin said. "Our study will be the best, you watch."

Julio looked at me. "So what's your idea?"

"It's weird."

"So tell."

I thought a moment. "Okay. Here's the

question: How come dogs got stink breath, and how can you make it better?"

Julio, Willy, and Rubin stared at me. Then they busted out laughing, rolling on the ground, holding their stomachs.

I should have kept my mouth shut.

Julio wiped his eyes. "I like it, I like it!"

"You do?"

"We can study stinks! We can collect them! Show that there are things way more stink than dog breath . . . you know, for props."

"Stinks can be props? How can you collect stinks?"

"I don't know. But gotta be a way, ah?"

I laughed. "Maybe there is."

Willy jumped in. "Stinkbugs could be a prop. We had those in California. Terrible smell. You can put one in a jar."

"Yeah," Rubin added. "And then you got stink eye and stink talk."

I slapped Rubin's arm. "You are so bazooks, Ruby-boy."

"Whatchoo stupits doing, making all this noise?"

I snapped up straight.

Tito Andrade, sixth-grade troublemaker, hovered over us. His friends Bozo and Frankie

Diamond stood on either side of him. With those three you could never tell what might happen. They could rob you, beat you up, embarrass you, or make you cry.

Bozo grinned. "Look how scared, ah, Tito?"

Tito snickered.

Me, Julio, Willy, and Rubin kept quiet. We

knew Tito was like a wasp. Sometimes he stung you, sometimes he just buzzed around your head making you sweat. Who knew?

Tito kicked my foot. "I axed you a question, Coco-punk, what's so funny?"

"Nothing."

"You just sitting here doing nothing? Like you stupit?"

"Yeah . . . I guess."

Julio, Willy, and Rubin kept quiet.

Frankie elbowed Tito. Lovey Martino, a sixth grader in tight jeans, was walking by.

Tito whistled at her. "Hoo, Lovey! Some nice, you! Come see Tito."

"Hanabata boy," Lovey said without looking at him.

I spurted out a laugh, then slapped my hand over my mouth. She'd just called him booger boy . . . to his face!

Tito must have liked it, because he grinned

22

and forgot all about us. He, Bozo, and Frankie Diamond walked off to follow Lovey Martino.

I let out my breath. "That was close."

"Yeah," Julio said. "Okay, back to collecting stinks. So we start with–"

"Breath, bad breath, bad-bad-bad breath."

"Zoo breath," Rubin added. "The kind makes your nose go bent."

Julio poked Rubin. "Since you got zoo breath yourself, you going be our first subject. Open you mouth."

"Hey," I said, elbowing Julio. "Look."

Tito, Bozo, and Frankie Diamond were heading back our way.

Julio jumped up. "Let's get out of here."

We ran off and ducked into the boys' bathroom.

Rubin wrinkled his nose. "Ho, man! Something died in here, or what?"

Julio nodded. "A new stink for our list around every corner."

That rotten boys'-room air and those stalls of peed-on toilet seats gave me an idea. "I just remembered something. I got the first big stink we can study."

"Couldn't smell more worse than this bathroom," Julio said.

I clamped my hand on his shoulder. "My house. Tomorrow. Ledward's bringing it over."

5

The Throne

The next day, Saturday, my mom's boyfriend, Ledward, and his big hairy pet pig, Blackie, came cruising down our street in Ledward's old army jeep. Blackie sat in the passenger seat, and a brand-new toilet sat in the back, bright white in the morning sun.

Streak's ears popped up like toast. She tilted her head and woofed.

Julio and I were lounging on the grass in his front yard.

Julio eyed Blackie. "Man, that just looks weird. A pig and a toilet in a jeep."

Today Ledward was taking our old toilet out and putting in a new one. I'd called him the night before and told him about our project. He thought it was hilarious.

The jeep puttered closer.

Streak studied Blackie and let loose barking.

"Hush." I pulled her close.

Ledward raised a finger off the steering wheel as he drove by.

I lifted my chin, Hey.

Ledward was a good guy. He was part Hawaiian, and six feet seven inches tall. Mom came up to just under his shoulder, if she stood on her toes. In platform shoes. On a box.

I jabbed Julio with my elbow. "So, here's the plan. Ledward is taking out the old toilet and putting in that new one."

"No kidding? You can just take a toilet off the floor?"

"That's what Ledward said."

"What happens with the . . . you know, the hole?"

"Got me."

Julio slapped his knee. "Genius, Calvin. This might be the worst stink you can find on the planet, ah?"

I grinned. "Let's go find out."

We hopped up and ran after the jeep as Ledward parked in our driveway. My house was the last one on the street. The river sparkled in the sun at the bottom of our sloping yard.

Ledward got out and dipped his head. "How's it going, boys?"

"Good," I said.

Julio gawked at Ledward's pig. Blackie was getting big. One day he'd grow tusks.

Streak whisked around the jeep, sniffing. Blackie didn't exactly smell like flowers. Hey, another stink to research. Pigs.

But today Blackie was spotless and gleaming in the sun.

"How come your pig is so clean today?" I asked.

Ledward put a finger to his lips. "Shhh. He doesn't know he's a you-know-what. In his mind he's a dog."

Julio started to laugh, but stopped. "Serious?"

Ledward chuckled. "I hosed him off."

Julio inched closer.

"He won't bite," I said.

But I had to admit Blackie did make you think twice about getting too close. I mean, he was once wild, and everyone knew that wild pigs could tear you up bad if they wanted to. Ledward had found Blackie when the pig was a baby, wandering alone in the jungle up near his house. Ledward said some hunter probably got Blackie's mama.

Ledward read my mind. "Blackie's as friendly as a tired old dog."

Blackie grunted and Julio jumped back.

Ledward untied the ropes around the new toilet. "Meet your new throne."

"Throne?"

"Like where the king sits."

I laughed at the picture in

my head: a king wearing a crown, sitting on the pot. "What do you do with the hole when you take out the old one?"

Ledward looked sideways at me. "Hole?"

"Where the . . . the stuff goes after you flush it."

"Ah, the sewer pipe. I show you. Little bit stink, but."

"Perfect," Julio said. "We're studying stinks."

Ledward chuckled. "That's what Calvin said."

He made a loop with a rope and slipped it around Blackie's neck. "Usually he won't run away because he's basically lazy. But better to be sure, ah?"

Since Blackie was too big to hop out of the jeep by himself, Ledward had to heft him down. The veins in Ledward's neck popped up like ropes. "Ooof!" he grunted.

Streak darted away and circled back, ears perked.

Blackie blinked, then huffed, like a sneeze mixed with a grunt. He stood almost to my waist.

"Let's find Blackie some shade and water," Ledward said. "After that, we go to work."

Ledward tied Blackie to the spigot under Darci's bedroom window. He filled Streak's water bowl and glanced at Streak. "You two can share, ah?"

Streak settled on the grass, tongue drooping in the heat.

Ledward went back to the jeep and got something wrapped in newspaper. "Aku head. For the dog."

He tossed the tuna head on the grass. Its mouth was open and the big black eye stared up at the sun. Streak snapped it up and took it down the slope toward the river. She loved fish heads.

Ledward wiped his hands on his shorts. "You boys ready to see what's under that toilet?"

6

The Hole

Ledward put his big arms around the toilet and lugged it off the backseat. "You boys grab my toolbox and hold the door open."

Julio got the toolbox.

I ran to the screen door and held it back.

Ledward squeezed by. We followed him in. "Stella! Darci!" I called. "Ledward's here!"

Mom worked Saturdays at Macy's on the other side of the island. She had ordered the new toilet, but she didn't know Ledward had picked it up and was putting it in today. He wanted it to be a surprise.

Stella was on her knees sorting laundry in Darci's room when Ledward huffed by. Darci's room was a mess, and Mom had asked Stella to help her clean it. Mom had also asked Stella to see if her lost black leather sandal was in there somewhere.

Stella glanced over her shoulder as we walked by.

"New toilet!" I said.

Darci scrambled up. "I want to see!"

Stella tried to grab her. "You come right back, you hear? I haven't got all day!"

Darci flattened Julio against the wall as she sped by. "I want to see! I want to see!"

Ledward eased the new toilet down in Mom's bathroom. "These things are fragile, believe it or not."

I squeezed into the bathroom next to Darci. "Can me and Julio help?"

"Of course," Ledward said. "You boys should know how a toilet works."

I grabbed a wrench out of Ledward's toolbox and handed it to him. "Let's do it."

"First we got to turn off the water."

Ledward turned the knob on a valve behind the tank. He flushed the toilet, then took the lid off the tank and sucked up the remaining water with a sponge.

"See this," he said, pointing to a copper tube behind the tank. "That's your water supply line, how the water gets into the tank. After I disconnect it we can lift this beast out of here."

Darci squatted for a better view. Stella scowled from the hall.

Ledward disconnected the water line, cranked off the tank bolts, and lifted the tank off the bowl. We moved back as he set it on the floor. "Now for the good part."

He took a big rag from his back pocket and spread it out on the bathroom floor. "Okay, junior plumbers. Ready?"

"Ready!" we said.

Ledward squatted and unbolted the bowl from the floor. He handed me the wrench. "Here we go."

Gently, he rocked the bowl back and forth. "Breaking the seal," he said. He stood, got a good grip, and lifted the toilet bowl away.

We all pushed back.

"Sits on a gasket," Ledward said, showing

us the goopy brown waxy stuff on the bottom of the toilet. "You don't want to get this on your floor. Hard to clean up."

He set the bowl on the rag, then squatted. "This is your sewer pipe."

We squeezed close to look down the hole in the floor.

"Eeeww! Eeeww! Stink! Stink! Stink!" Darci gasped.

I yanked my T-shirt up over my nose.

Darci staggered back and crab-walked her way out of the bathroom.

"Ho, man!" Julio yelped.

Ledward pointed his chin. "Grab that big rag."

I handed it to him and he balled it up and stuffed it into the sewer pipe. "That . . . is what's under your toilet."

Even with the rag in the pipe I could smell it through my T-shirt. I wanted to get out of there so bad my hands began to sweat.

Stella gagged in the hall. "Ack! Close your mouth, Calvin. I can smell your breath all the way out here."

Julio laughed and I shoved him out of the bathroom. "Let me out!"

As we banged past Stella I huffed out a gust of my best zoo breath right in her face.

She staggered back. "You moron!"

We stumbled out the screen door and sprawled on the grass, laughing like fools.

"No stink can beat that one," Julio said.

"Maybe, maybe not," I said.

"What can be worse?"

"I've got ideas."

7

Pink-and-Black Spies

We got up to check on Blackie. He was asleep, flies sitting on his closed eyes.

Streak sat nearby. She'd finished the fish head, bones and all.

"Go smell your dog's breath now," Julio said. "See if it's worse than that hole."

"Sure, right after you kiss her on the lips."

Julio laughed. "That was so funny, what you did to Stella."

"I'll pay for it, too. But she started it."

Julio raised his chin toward Blackie. "Look. The pig's mouth is open."

"So?"

"So this is your chance to smell pig breath. Go on, see if it's more worse than your dog's."

I looked at Blackie. Julio was right. How often can you smell pig breath? I crept close and did it. Blackie slept on.

"Bad, but not deadly."

We headed out to the street. Streak popped up and followed us.

"Now what?" Julio said.

Just then something moved in the bushes. A flash of color. Pink. And black. Streak's ears shot up.

I bumped Julio over to the side of the road. "We got company," I whispered.

"Where?"

"In the bushes. Don't look."

"Who is it?"

"Spies."

He started to look, but I grabbed him. "Listen. When I say *now,* we turn and run right at them. They won't have time to get away."

"Who's they?"

"I don't know."

"What if it's Tito?"

"Tito doesn't wear pink."

"Pink?"

"Ready? *Now!*"

Whoever it was, was smart. The bushes shivered as the spies raced out toward the golf

course on the other
side.

Streak barked and ran into
the jungle. Julio and I stumbled after
her. I held my hands up to block my face from
low branches. Ahead I saw a pink shirt, and a
black one.

"Who is it?" Julio called. "Can you see?"

"No, but there's two of them."

They were too far ahead to catch, but
once we got out on the golf course we
could see who they were. I hoped there
weren't any golfers, or worse, the jeep
guys, who roamed the fairways looking
for kids to chase off the course.

"Streak!" I called.

She turned and came back. I grabbed her collar so she wouldn't run out of the jungle. "Good girl."

We stopped at the edge of the seventh green. A golfer was in the sand trap, waiting to hit out of it. But he and another guy were looking down the fairway at the two escaping spies.

Julio and I backed into the bushes. Streak growled. "Shhh," I whispered.

"Did you see who it was?" Julio asked.

"I think so. Let's get out of here."

We headed back through the jungle and out onto our street. I let Streak go and she took off after a mongoose that scurried across the road down by my house.

"So who was it?" Julio asked.

"You'll never in your whole life guess."

"Tito?"

"Nope. Shayla and Maya!"

"For real?"

"Pretty sure."

But was I? It wasn't like Maya to spy on us.

Shayla, yes, but not Maya. "I wonder what they were up to."

"Has to be their project. Why else would Maya be with Shayla?"

"Hey," I said. "If they're working on their project, then you owe me a bag of dried shrimp."

"Okay, fine, but how come they were spying on us?"

"Maybe they weren't. Maybe they were just hiding."

"But . . . why?"

We headed to Julio's house and sat on the grass in his front yard. From there I could see Maya's house. Like always, Maya's black cat, Zippy, was sleeping out in the street.

I leaned back on my elbows. "Sooner or later they got to show."

"Sooner," Julio said. "Look."

Maya and Shayla were heading out of Maya's garage, only they were dressed different. "Huh," Julio said. "I thought one was pink and one was black."

Now I was worried. Was I wrong? No, I can tell those two from a mile away. "They changed."

"Sneaky," Julio said.

Maya and Shayla looked our way and waved.

"Sneaky is right. Pretending nothing happened."

They headed up the street in the opposite direction. I could hear them laughing.

Something was up.

8

Pot of Tears

Later, me and Julio tried to get up close to his brother's pet white rat and check its breath. But it bit Julio's nose, so we gave that up.

"We need a zoo," I said as we headed out of his house. "I bet they got all kinds of stink breath there."

"Zoo breath."

"Prob'ly monkeys got the worst."

"How come?"

"They always eating bugs from each other's heads."

"That's weird, man."

"Not as weird as that," I said, pointing my chin down the street. "A cat with a death wish."

Zippy the black blob was still sleeping out in the middle of the road. Someday he was going to get squished. "Let's go see if a cat's breath is as bad as a dog's."

Julio shrugged. "They eat mice."

"And they always licking their okoles."

"Eeew, butt breath."

We headed toward the black blob.

"Hey, Zipster," I said.

Zippy stretched and looked up at us.

I squatted. "Open up. Julio wants to smell your breath."

"Your turn," Julio said. "I already got bit once."

I got closer to Zippy. "Okay . . . let me have it."

Zippy rolled over on his back. I took a quick sniff and jumped back when he clawed at me. "Yuck!"

"Bad?" Julio asked.

"Cat food breath."

We headed back to my house.

Ledward's jeep was still in the driveway. When Mom got home I was thinking maybe I'd ask her if Julio could sleep over so we could come up with fresh ideas.

We headed into the garage. Julio stopped. "Ha! Look what your dog did!"

Streak was lounging on the mat by the kitchen door, bits of rubber between her paws. She slapped her tail on the ground and looked up. Part of one of Mom's rubber slippers hung from the side of her mouth.

"Jeese Louise, Streak! You want to get sent back to the Humane Society *tonight*? Gimme that!"

I yanked what was left of the slipper out of her mouth and scooped up the shredded pieces, then tossed it all into the garbage can.

Streak looked up with a goofy dog grin, Heh-heh.

"You are *so* lucky I came home before Mom did, because you'd be history if she saw what you were doing. *History!*"

Streak yawned, her eyes turning to slits.

Julio laughed his head off.

Inside, Ledward, Darci, and Stella were standing around in the kitchen.

"What's going on?" I asked.

Darci beamed. "We're waiting for Mom. We're going to surprise her!"

Stella sat on a stool at the counter gazing out the window. "Shock her, is more like it."

"Come see," Darci said, grabbing my hand.

Julio wagged his eyebrows. "Let's do it."

Ledward had covered the new toilet with an old sheet. Darci lifted it up. There was a big red Christmas bow stuck to the seat. "Wow," I said.

Someone had cleaned up Mom's entire bathroom. There was even a vase of flowers. The place sparkled.

We waited in the kitchen.

Darci had invited her stuffed parrot, Petey, there to see it.

When Mom finally came home, we cheered.

"What's all this?" she said.

Streak tried to squeeze in the door behind her, but Mom nudged her back into the garage with her foot.

Mom pecked Ledward on the cheek.

"Welcome home," he said.

"You don't know how welcome it is. What a busy day at the store!" She sighed. "Hi, Julio."

Julio lifted his chin.

"Okay, family," Mom said, giving me and Darci quick hugs. "What's going on here?"

Darci tugged at her dress. "We have a surprise for you."

"Yeah, Mom," I said. "You gotta see it."

Stella rolled her eyes like, Big deal.

Mom dropped her keys and purse on the counter. "I could use a surprise."

Ledward stood behind her and massaged her shoulders.

Mom closed her eyes.

"Come," Ledward said, stopping. "We show you."

Mom grabbed his hand and put it back on her shoulder. "Can't we just stay here a minute?"

But Darci was too excited. "Come see, come see!"

Mom followed us down the hall.

"Close your eyes," Ledward said.

We squeezed in close, even Stella.

Darci jumped up and down. "Open your eyes, Mom!"

Ledward pulled the sheet away.

"Oh, my," Mom whispered. She put a fist to her lips and looked at us. Tears swelled in her eyes.

Tears? Over a toilet? Didn't she like it?

Mom knelt down and gathered me and Darci in. She gave us the biggest hug ever. "You don't know, you just don't know . . . I am so lucky to have so much help, I just love you all to pieces."

Stella watched us a second, then turned and walked away.

"You like it?" Ledward asked.

"I like you," she said, and reached for his hand.

"Can Julio sleep over, Mom?" I asked.

"Of course he can . . . but only after you shovel up all your dog's little treasures in the yard."

"Sure, Mom."

Julio and I started to leave.

"Wait!" Darci said, and I stopped. "I forgot. I talked to Dad today. He called. He said he'd call again later to talk to you."

I glanced at Mom. Her happy face became a frown. She tried to turn it back into a smile.

"Go," Ledward said, giving me a little shove. "I come get you if he calls back."

Julio and I headed for the pooper scooper.

9

Treasures

Streak was lounging on the doormat. "Hey, girl," I said. "Come help us clean up your mess."

I reached down and scratched her under the chin. She liked that. "Try to stay out of trouble, okay? Mom's about five minutes from sending you to the moon."

Julio snorted. "Impossible for that mutt to stay out of trouble."

I laughed. "True."

I grabbed the shovel. Crusty brown stuff was dried out on the blade.

Julio pointed at it with his chin. "What's that?"

"Here, smell it and tell me."

Julio jerked back and ran out of the garage into the sunlight. "Hey, listen," he said. "I got to go tell my mom I'm staying at your place tonight . . . and get my sleeping bag, too."

"Oh no you don't. Help me do this first. Then I'll go with you."

"Fine. But no way I'm shoveling up that stink stuff."

I grinned. "Watch your step."

Streak followed us out into the yard.

I spotted something black on the lawn. I went over to see what it was. "Oh no," I whispered.

Julio shook his head. "Can't salvage that!"

I looked over my shoulder. No one was

looking out the window. I picked up Mom's chewed-up black leather sandal and flung it into the bushes. If she ever saw it Streak would be in big trouble, and me, too.

"Dang dog," I said to Streak. "I can get Mom new rubber slippers. They don't cost much. But sandals? Do you know how hard it is to make money?"

Streak yawned.

I sighed and looked around. The long, un-cut grass was so full of hidden dog treasures that I didn't know where to start. So I just went hunting, scooping stuff up and flipping it all into the bushes between our house and the river. "Boing!"

Julio winced. "Remind me never to go in *those* bushes."

"Got that right."

I scooped more poop, thinking about what Dad did with Chewy. That mutt had bad breath, too. No, not bad. More like death. I laughed.

"What?"

"You remember our old dog, Chewy?"

"Yeah, sort of."

"My dad used to brush his teeth."

"For real?"

I nodded. "With a toothbrush. Chewy made faces and smacked his lips. When he was done, Dad squirted his mouth out with a hose."

"Weird."

"Yeah . . . but funny, too."

Now I was starting to miss Dad and Chewy. Usually I didn't think about them. They'd been gone a long time; I was almost six when they left. At the time, I just thought that was how it was. Dads moved on. No big deal.

But it was a big deal. I just kept it to myself. Easier that way.

I blew out a long breath. Then I wondered if Chewy's old dog toothpaste and dog shampoo were still around. Dad used to keep it all under the sink in the kitchen.

"Here," I said. I handed Julio the shovel and ran toward the house. "Finish up. I have to check something."

Julio took the shovel. Then realized what he'd just done. "Hey! I ain't flipping no dog doo."

"Boing!" I shouted over my shoulder.

"You owe me, punk!"

"I'll pay you in friendship!"

10

Dog-Doo City

"Hi, Mom," I said, running into the kitchen.

She was standing at the counter looking at the newspaper. Ledward was outside sweeping the patio.

Without looking up Mom said, "That was quick. Did you get all the–"

"Yeah, Mom. I'm on it."

"Thank you."

"Yeah, sure," I said, dropping to my knees. I checked under the kitchen sink. There it was, hidden way in back. Bingo! Dog toothpaste, dog shampoo, and an old brush with some of Chewy's hair still in it.

I sat back on my heels.

Dang. Now I really missed them.

"What are you looking for?" Mom asked.

I put the brush back and kept the shampoo and toothpaste. The stuff had to be as old as dirt. I shrugged. Give it a try.

"Calvin?"

"Oh, uh . . . I was thinking about . . . giving Streak a bath or something. Look, Chewy's old shampoo is still here."

"Throw it out. But a bath is a great idea. We can get you some new shampoo."

I opened the container and smelled it. "Smells fine to me."

"I don't know, Calvin. Everything has a shelf life."

"A what?"

"It's old. Toss it."

I took the shampoo and the toothpaste out to the garage, but I didn't toss them. I set them down by some old paint cans. I didn't have to give her a bath right now.

When I walked out of the garage, I saw them again.

The spies.

But this time I could tell who it was for sure. Maya and Shayla, sneaking around in the bushes.

Those bushes. Dog-doo city.

"Julio," I whispered, coming up to him, casual-like.

He scowled at me, the shovel loaded to the max.

"Wait," I whispered. "Don't toss it. Look. Maya and Shayla are spying again."

Julio's eyes shifted. "Where are they?"

"In the bushes."

"What bushes?"

I grinned.

"Not," he said with a gleam in his eye.

I nodded. "Shhh."

We waited, listening, Julio holding the loaded shovel, both of us trying not to crack up.

A shriek came from the bushes. "Aww! Ick, ick, *ick!*"

Julio spurted out a laugh and spilled the loaded shovel near my bare feet.

I jumped out of the way.

I heard Maya trying to quiet Shayla.

Bits of color flashed through the bushes as they raced out of there, trying not to be seen.

Julio scooped up the fallen mess and flipped it into the bushes. "Boing!" He flung the

shovel toward the
house. We stum-
bled over to
some clean
grass and
fell, holding
our sides and
laughing so hard it
hurt.

Fifteen minutes later, still grinning, we
went to Julio's house to get his sleeping
bag. Down the street Maya and Shayla
were in Maya's yard, squirting their
feet with a hose.

Julio and I cracked up all over again.

Ho, man, if this wasn't a perfect day, I
didn't know what was.

11

Putrid

We still had some good sunlight left, so me, Julio, and Darci decided to give Streak a bath. Maybe I could make her smell good, look good, and act good. Then Mom and Stella wouldn't have so much to complain about.

Julio grabbed the old dog shampoo and I got out Darci's inflatable swimming pool and blew it up. "Ho!" I said, feeling dizzy. "Okay. Darci, bring the hose and turn on the water."

As we filled the pool, Streak came over for a drink.

Julio leaned down to pet her. "This isn't your water bowl, you lolo dog."

I turned off the water. "Okay, Streak. Time to clean you up!"

I lifted her into the pool. She cocked her head like, What are we doing here?

But she seemed to like it, and sat down in the water.

"See?" I said. "It's nice."

The front door slapped. Ledward waved and headed around the side of the house to get Blackie, who'd had a long day of shady rest. A minute later he was back, Blackie huffing along behind him. "I think he likes it here."

Ledward lifted Blackie onto the front seat of the jeep, got in, started it up, and drove off, giving the horn a toot. Blackie's ears bent back in the breeze.

"Crazy," Julio said.

Me and Julio went back to scooping handfuls of water over Streak's head. She liked it. "Good girl," I said.

Julio gave Streak a pat. "You're helping us, dog. Mr. Purdy will give us an A-plus for discovering how to get rid of your stink."

I grabbed Chewy's old shampoo. "Yeah, but we're supposed to be discovering how come she got stink *breath.*"

Darci looked up. "Well, that's easy, Calvin."

"What's easy?"

"Why she has bad breath."

I looked at her. "Why?"

"It's Ledward's fault. He gives her fish heads."

I sat back. "You're right. The fish heads!"

Streak liked her bath so much she wouldn't leave the pool. I had to lift her out. She shook herself off all over us, but who cared? We were already soaked.

Julio sniffed Streak. "Still stinks."

"That's just wet dog smell," I said. "Whenever she comes out of the river she smells like that."

Streak rolled around in the grass. Luckily, it was the clean part. She pretty much did her business in one area of the yard.

"Come eat!" Stella called from the house.

We went in through the garage to the kitchen, the one place Streak could go in the house.

Mom and Stella were taking food out to the table, which was in the living room.

"Where'd Ledward go?" I asked.

"He'll be back in time for dessert. He had to run Blackie home. And he has to feed his dogs."

Ledward had a pig and four dogs. He must have to scoop poop, too, I thought. I hoped he had more than a shovel. Maybe a bulldozer.

"Yuck!" Stella snapped. "What stinks?"

I glanced at Streak. I sort of smelled something, too.

Mom looked at us.

Julio took a step away. "I think she got into something after the bath."

Stella gagged, going for drama. "That's putrid. What *is* it?"

Mom pointed toward the door. "Take her out. Now!"

I snapped to it. "Come on, girl. I'll bring you your dinner."

I opened the door to the garage and nudged Streak out.

Me and Julio followed. I flipped on the garage light. It was getting dark.

"Man!" I said. "She rolled in something. Dead toad?"

Julio bent close. "Yeah, prob'ly."

"Dang things are everywhere. We got to hose her off."

I looked at Streak. "You have to get clean and stay clean, girl. Mom is going to make me give you back, and if she does that . . . well, I'm just going to have to . . . to . . . run away, that's all. You and me both."

Streak gave me that look dogs give you when they know they've done something bad.

I squatted to pet her head. "I know, I know. You can't help it."

Streak licked my hand.

Julio squirted us both with the hose.

12

Little JohNNy CocoNut

After Ledward had come back for dessert, the phone rang.

I grabbed it. "Hello?"

"Calvin?"

Dad.

I stretched the phone cord around the

kitchen corner and sat on the floor by our dining room table. Darci and Julio were watching TV. Stella had gone somewhere with her boyfriend, Clarence. Mom and Ledward were sitting in the dark out on the patio.

I looked at the dirt under my fingernails, as if what I was supposed to say might be hidden there.

"Calvin? Is that you?"

"Uh . . . yeah . . . I'm here."

I twisted the mangled phone cord around my fingers.

"Well, how the heck are you, son? We haven't spoken in ages, and . . . well, I guess that's mostly my fault, huh? But you know how busy I've been at the club, and all."

Think, think.

"Yeah . . . sure," I said. In the background I heard a yap. My blank head filled with memories. "Was that Chewy?"

"Sure was. Want to say hi?"

"Yeah, Dad, put the phone by his ear."

"Hang on." I could hear Dad calling Chewy over. Dad fumbled with the phone, then said, "Go ahead. He's listening."

"Chewy!" I said. "How's it going, boy? You miss me?"

There was a soft whine and some breathing.

"Yeah, boy, I miss you, too," I said. "You like Las Vegas?"

Chewy barked, and Dad laughed.

"What are you doing, sweetie?" I heard someone in the background say. Marissa? Dad's wife?

"It's Calvin," Dad said. "He's talking to Chewy."

"Oh, how sweet," she said.

Dad took the phone back. "You made Chewy's day, Calvin. I haven't seen him this excited in a long time."

"I found his toothpaste."

"Huh?"

"Chewy's toothpaste. I found it under the sink. And his old dog shampoo. Remember?"

Dad laughed. "Your mother should have thrown that stuff out years ago."

"I have a dog now. Her name is Streak."

"That's great, Calvin. Great name, too. What kind of a dog is it?"

"Poi dog . . . you know, a mix. She's bigger than Chewy. She's black and white, and the best dog ever . . . like Chewy is."

Dad chuckled. "Guess you and I are pretty lucky, huh?"

"Yeah."

Dad covered the phone and mumbled something to Marissa. "I'll be quick," he said, taking his hand away. "Hey, listen, I got to run in a sec. I just wanted to hear your voice and see how you're doing."

"I'm fine, Dad."

"Great! Well, gotta run. We'll talk again soon. I'll call. You take good care of that dog, now."

"I will. You want to talk to Darci?"

"We talked earlier."

"Okay."

"Mind your mom and stay cool, bud. I'm thinking of you."

"Sure, Dad. Bye."

He started talking to Marissa before he hung up. I sat looking at the phone. Hearing Chewy, hearing Dad. I hadn't even known I'd missed them. But I sure did now.

When I put the phone back in the kitchen I saw Mom and Ledward on the patio. Mom waved for me to come out. I slid open the screen door, then quickly shut it to keep the mosquitoes out.

"Was that who I think it was?" Mom asked.

"Yeah."

Mom nodded. "Did you have a good talk?"

"I guess."

I looked down. I could feel grains of sand under my bare feet on the polished cement patio. You couldn't get away from sand. Even after Ledward swept.

I'd hardly talked to Dad at all, and Mom knew it.

"I talked to Chewy," I said, looking up.

Mom sighed. "At least there was that, then."

"Yeah, but . . . Julio's here, and . . ."

"Go on, Cal. I'm just glad he called."

I nodded and left.

13

Captured

I always slept on the top bunk, so Julio took the bottom, which was usually Streak's bed. That was why Julio brought his sleeping bag. Who wanted to sleep in dog fuzz?

Streak curled up on the floor.

Julio pushed up on my mattress with his

feet. "Hey. So what are we doing about the project? We need a good thought."

"I don't even have a bad one."

"Yeah, but we got some examples to show there's stinks worse than dog breath, ah?"

"Well, yeah . . . but what do we have to show for it? I mean like props."

"We should have collected them."

I leaned over the edge of my bunk. "Collected stinks?"

"That's our project, right?"

"Yeah, but . . . collect *stinks*?"

"What you going use that jar on your desk for?"

"I don't know. I just saved it, is all."

"Good. We can use it."

"For what?"

He was silent a minute. "Dog doo could be one example." Julio kicked me through the mattress again.

"Stop *doing* that!"

Julio laughed. "It would be a good prop,

ah? Am I right? Nobody would forget it."

I had to admit Julio was right. But if we brought dog doo in a jar to class we'd get sent to the principal's office. For sure.

Still. "I guess it would be good to have examples."

"Everyone will have them, prob'ly."

"Yeah."

I rolled back and looked up at Spidey in his web in the corner of the ceiling. He hadn't moved in weeks. Outside, the bufos down by the river started acting up. The noise they made was really loud. But I liked it. A mosquito sang in my ear and I batted it away. That was a sound I hated.

"Ah, man!" Julio made choking sounds. "Ack! Ack!"

I looked down over the edge of the bunk. "What?"

His face was covered by his pillow. "Your dog wen' fut!"

I caught a whiff and rolled

back onto my bed, cracking up. Julio was right down there in the thick of it.

He kicked the bottom of my bunk hard. "Not funny!"

I flew up an inch, still laughing.

"Blech! That is so bad!"

"Hey, catch *that* in the jar. It can be a prop."

Julio popped up, grabbed the jar on my desk, and took the lid off.

"That was a *joke,*" I said.

"No, it's a good idea. How you catch a fut?"

I looked down. "Well, go right down by

Streak's okole and scoop it up, quick before you breathe it all in."

Julio captured some stink air, clamped the lid down, and jumped back in bed. "Got it!"

"Right on, brah," I said. "Right on!"

He kicked my bunk again.

Awhile later, I heard Ledward outside. His jeep was parked on the grass near my window. I'd turned out the light, but me and Julio weren't asleep. We'd been talking about sneaking out and rowing my skiff up the river in the dark.

"Boy," Ledward called through the screen. "You sleeping?"

I rolled onto my elbows and looked out the window. "No."

"Your friend in there with you?"

"Yeah."

"Good, good."

He stood just outside the window. "You okay?"

"Well . . . sure . . . why wouldn't I be?"

"I just thought . . . well, you had that phone call. You looked little bit down."

The bufos were getting quieter now, heading deeper into the night. I rolled onto my back, looking up at the dark ceiling. "I'm fine," I said.

"Good. But listen . . . you ever need to talk about anything, you come see me, okay?"

What did he mean? Talk about what?

"So," Ledward said. "You boys have a good night."

I listened to the jeep rumble away until there was no sound but the whisper of bufos hopping in the grass down by the water.

"Hey," Julio said.

"Yeah?"

"What's more worse, dog breath or dog fut?"

14

Disgusting

I woke up the next morning and peeked at my clock on the windowsill. Just after noon. Still early, I thought, stretching. But I didn't want to waste the day.

I slid down from my bunk and shook Julio. "Hey."

He groaned. His pillow was over his head to block the light.

Streak was curled by his feet. She raised her head.

"Julio, get up."

He mumbled something I couldn't understand.

"Come on. We got an experiment to do."

He lifted the pillow off his face. "We do?"

"Yeah, remember? It was your idea: find out what's worse, dog breath or dog fut."

Julio dropped the pillow back on his face. "Gotta be kidding."

"Get up! We need stuff for our project."

"All right, all right." He sat up and rubbed his face. Streak jumped up and licked him.

He shoved her away. "Git, you pest."

"Smell her breath," I said. "See if it's worse. Go. Smell it now."

"Not before breakfast."

"Look," I said, scratching Streak's chin. "You hurt her feelings."

"Pssh."

Stella was at the kitchen sink, gargling with her back to us. A bottle of blue mouthwash sat on the counter. She jumped when we barged in, catching her doing something she should have been doing in the bathroom.

She turned the water on and spat into the sink. "Where do you get off, sneaking up on people like that?"

"We didn't sneak up," I said. "We just came in the kitchen."

Julio stood behind me. He was scared of her.

"Where's Mom?" I said.

"What am I, your personal answering machine?"

"All I did was ask."

"Well, don't," she said on her way out of the kitchen.

I opened the fridge and grabbed the milk,

then got a box of Frosted Mini-Wheats and two bowls.

Julio started breathing again. "Man, is she always that friendly in the morning?"

"Now you know what I have to live with."

We ate Mini-Wheats at the counter by the window. The sun was so bright outside it made me squint.

When we were done we went out through the garage. Streak jumped up and followed us. I tossed her a couple Mini-Wheats, then dropped a scoop of dry dog food in her food dish and filled up her water bowl, which was bone dry.

Streak dug in, looking up at us as she crunched.

"Okay," I said to Julio. "You ready for the experiment?"

"Nope."

"Good. Let's get that jar."

We had a serious project going on here. We needed to do some detecting.

I got the jar. "So, who's going to do it?"

"It's your dog."

I was hoping he wouldn't say that. "Fine. You take notes."

"I take um in my mind."

"You got a mind?"

We crouched on the grass. Streak sat between us.

I set the jar down. I couldn't help wondering what it smelled like inside. I half laughed. This was really dumb.

I looked at the jar. Looked at Streak. Shook my head. "Can't do it."

"Come on, Calvin. It's research, remember? Do it for Mr. Purdy."

I picked up the jar. Put my hand on the lid. This was too disgusting. Even for me.

I set the jar back on the grass and looked at Julio.

"Not me," he said. "No way."

Streak ran off to nose around in the grass down by the river.

The sun burned through my T-shirt.

I looked up and saw Stella pass through the living room in the big front window.

Stella, who could make my dog go away by complaining to Mom.

And what was I doing about it?

Catching stinks in a jar.

15

Lips

There had to be a solution for Streak.

So, what was the problem? Fixing her breath.

But really, the problem wasn't Streak. It was Mom and Stella, who couldn't tell the difference between a regular stink and a good one.

Just then, my first good thought popped into my head. "Forget that jar," I said. "Streak! Come here, girl!"

She came running.

I put my arm around her. She was sun-warm.

"I got it, Julio! Ho, yeah! You know how Stella was in the kitchen gargling? We can give some of *that* stuff to Streak."

Julio laughed. "This I got to see! Coco-clown and his gargling dog."

"Well, maybe she just laps it up."

Julio shook his head. "You getting desperate, my friend."

"Wait," I said. "Be right back."

I ran into the house and grabbed one of the cereal bowls Julio and I had used. I poured some of Stella's blue mouthwash into it. It smelled good. If this worked Streak would have breath that smelled just like Stella's, and how could she complain about that?

Genius!

I ran back out and set the bowl on the

grass. I grinned. Wouldn't it be funny if Streak really could gargle? But wait. What if she just drank it up? Would it hurt her? Naah. It'd only be a sip.

Streak headed right for it. I grabbed her. "Hang on, girl. First Julio has to test your breath so we can see if this makes it better."

Julio grinned. "Nice try."

"Fine." I faked a scowl. "Streak. Open up."

I put my face close to hers. She licked my

nose. Streak just smelled like a dog. I didn't know what Mom and Stella were complaining about.

"Stink?" Julio asked.

"Little bit fishy, but . . . no."

"Huh."

"You try," I said. "Just to be sure."

He hesitated, then leaned in. "Yack!" he spat, wiping his lips when Streak licked them.

"So?" I asked.

"That was sick."

Streak, meanwhile, lapped up the mouth-wash.

"Hey!" I pulled her away.

Streak worked her mouth, like she had something stuck to her tongue.

"I don't think she liked it."

"Check her now," Julio said.

I did. She'd never smelled so good.

"WHAT are you DOING?" someone snapped.

I jumped and fell back.

Stella hovered over us, looking down with

her hands on her hips. "Did you just smell that dog's breath?"

I shook my head. "No."

Stella grinned. "Did you kiss her?"

"NO!"

Stella threw her head back and laughed. She headed into the house, singing, "Calvin kissed her on the lips, now the dog is gonna get sick! Calvin kissed her on the—"

"STOP!"

The screen door slapped shut. I could hear her cackling, even in the house.

Darci ran to the window like, What's going on out there?

Mom called from the garage. "Calvin!"

I turned. "Yeah, Mom?"

"Could you come here a minute? There's something dead."

16

Something Dead

I headed over to Mom, still angry at Stella.

Mom put her hand on my shoulder. "A very bad smell drifted through my bedroom window all night long. Can you boys find out where it's coming from and remove it?"

"Sure, Mom." I grabbed the shovel from the garage in case we had to bury something.

Then I got an idea.

"Hey, Mom, I bet Streak can find it. She has a nose for stuff." The more good things I could say about Streak the better.

"I believe that one hundred percent, Cal."

Me, Julio, and Streak set out with our noses and the shovel.

I'd forgotten all about Stella until I saw her in the window making kissy faces at me.

I held up the pooper scooper shovel blade and pretended to lick it.

Her kissy face froze. "That is so disgusting!" she shouted, her voice muffled by the window.

Julio tapped my arm. "Look. I think your dog found it."

Just outside Mom's

window a dead toad lay bloated and maggoty on the grass. Streak crept up to it.

"No!" I said. "Come away from that."

Streak backed off.

Julio pulled his T-shirt up over his nose. "I bet that's what she rolled in. Man, that stinks."

I grunted and shoveled up the dead bufo. "Should we put it in a jar?"

"Sheese, Calvin! Toss that thing."

I catapulted it into the bushes. "Boing."

"You prob'ly should have buried it," Julio said. "Still going stink."

"Too late now. No way I'm going in those bushes looking for it."

Julio tapped my arm. "Check out who's here."

I turned to see.

Maya headed into the yard from the street. "Hey," she said. "What are you doing?"

"Scooping up dead stuff. What are *you* doing?"

"Nothing. I'm bored."

Julio glanced up the street. "Where's Shayla?"

"Home, I guess."

I squinted at her. "Why were you spying on us?"

Maya gave us a surprised, innocent look. "Spying?"

"You and Shayla. Spying by the golf course. Spying in the bushes."

She glanced at the dog-doo bushes and frowned. "You must be thinking of someone else. Why would we spy on you? I can just walk up and see you anytime I want."

Julio scoffed. "We saw it was you."

Maya shook her head. "A case of mistaken identity."

This was going nowhere. "Okay, fine," I said. "We know it was you, but forget it. What are you and Shayla working on for your research project?"

Maya smiled. "Secret."

"Come on," Julio said. "We won't steal it."

"Tell me yours first."

I shook my head. "Can't. Secret."

"Well, there you go," Maya said.

We looked at each other.

"So," Maya said.

"So," I said back.

Julio stepped in. "So this: How come Shayla was over at your house? You like her now, or what?"

Maya grinned. "She likes Calvin."

"Shuddup!" I said.

Maya laughed. "She's not so bad."

Julio's jaw dropped. "Not so bad? Are you kidding? She's snoopy. She's annoying. She's a pest."

"She's kind of sad."

That jolted me. "*Sad?* Why?"

Maya bunched her lips. "No brothers and sisters, no friends, really . . . and her dad just left to go live somewhere else for a while."

"How come?" Julio asked.

Maya shrugged.

I could understand the part about Shayla's dad leaving. "Too bad," I said.

Julio nodded. "Well . . . she's smart, I guess. Even if she is weird."

"She's not weird," Maya said. "And don't talk about my research partner like that."

Julio put his hands up in surrender.

Maya punched him in the gut. But not hard.

"Hey!"

"Sorry to break up such a fun time," I said. "But me and Julio got our project to do."

"So what is it?"

I smiled. "What's yours?"

Maya scoffed and headed away. Over her shoulder she said, "Whatever yours is, ours is better! In fact, if I was you two I wouldn't even come to school on Tuesday!"

"What does that mean?"

She laughed, and jogged up the street.

"I didn't like the sound of that."

Streak barked once, then cocked her head.

Julio snorted. "Streak didn't like it, either."

17

Rare Air

On Monday Mr. Tanaka (the rock star librarian who had musical instruments set up all over the school library) let me, Julio, Willy, and Rubin work on our projects during recess. We had things to look up, ideas to nail down. We hunched around a table.

"You guys have any props?" Willy asked.

I reached into my backpack, pulled out the jar, and held it up.

"An empty jar?"

I grinned at him and flicked my eyebrows. "It just looks empty."

Rubin frowned, squinting at the jar.

I nudged Willy's knee with mine. "What you guys doing? Still the manga books?"

Willy nodded. "They're kind of weird."

Rubin slouched in his chair, his leg

bouncing. He lifted his chin at the jar on the table. "So what's it for?"

"This," Julio said, tapping the lid with a finger, "is for what's inside it."

Rubin frowned. "It's empty."

"No, no, no," Julio said. "Inside this jar is . . . rare air."

I laughed.

Willy looked closer. "Really?"

Julio picked up the jar and peered into it. "You can hardly get this kind of air, it's so rare. It came from a special place."

"Pshh!" Rubin snorted.

"No, really, Ruby. You want to smell it?"

"Aw, man!" I said, screeching my chair back.

Willy slapped my arm with the back of his hand and nodded toward Mr. Tanaka, who was giving me squinty librarian stink eye.

"Sure, I'll smell it," Rubin whispered, leaning close.

Julio gave Rubin a grave face. "I don't

know, Ruby. If you smell it, it will go inside your lungs and we won't get it back. Then what will me and Calvin do?"

Rubin chewed on his thumbnail. "Well . . . can't you just go get more where you got it from?"

Julio nodded, as if considering that. "Sure . . . yeah, we could do that, right, Calvin?"

I shook my head. "I don't know, Julio. It was a dangerous place. But sure. Let him smell it."

Julio put the jar close to Rubin's nose. "You ready?"

"Ready."

"Take a deep breath when I open it, because it's going to fly out fast and you might miss it if you don't suck it in quick."

"Yeah-yeah, let it loose."

Julio unscrewed the lid. "Now!"

Julio lifted the lid away and Rubin took a huge breath, his nose nearly inside the jar.

He sat back and considered it.

Julio raised his eyebrows. "Well?"

"Well what?" Rubin said, clearly disappointed. "It was just like regular air. But . . . kind of . . . swampy?"

I burst out laughing.

Mr. Tanaka tipped back in his chair and crossed his arms.

I stopped laughing. Tried to, anyway.

Mr. Tanaka shook his head and let the front legs of his chair drop back to the floor. "Knuckleheads," he mumbled.

Willy picked up the empty jar. "So what kind of air was it?"

Julio looked from Rubin to Willy, Willy to Rubin.

Building up the suspense.

He leaned close. "Dog fut," he said.

Rubin squinted. Then he got it.

"Ahhhh!" He grabbed his throat and ran outside to gulp in some fresh air. "You stupit!" he shouted.

Me and Julio fell out of our chairs and rolled on the floor. So funny! Even Willy cracked up.

Mr. Tanaka stood and pointed to the door.

We gathered up our stuff and Rubin's and headed out.

"Bozos," Mr. Tanaka mumbled as we filed by. But he was grinning. "Now I can say I've seen everything a school librarian can possibly see."

Julio flicked his eyebrows. "We got more if you—"

"Git!" Mr. Tanaka said.

18

Sulfur

Streak came slinking out of the garage when Darci and I got home from school. I squatted down and sat on my heels.

"Ho, man! What now?"

Even Darci puckered up. "What is that smell, Calvin?"

"Barf. Look."

She must have gotten into something down at the river that made her sick.

Streak inched up closer, her head hanging down. She knew she was in trouble. Luckily Mom was at work. And Stella wasn't home yet.

"You just can't stay out of trouble, can you?"

Streak barked.

"Time for another bath, you mangy mutt."

"Can I help?" Darci asked.

I nodded. "Sure. Go change. We're gonna get wet."

Darci ran into the house.

I unfolded the crinkly pool and popped out the air valve. As I was blowing it up I saw something green near the paint cans.

"Ah, man. Not Petey."

I picked up Darci's stuffed parrot. Streak had been gnawing on it. Luckily, she hadn't ripped it apart, but it was crusty with dried dog spit.

I took the pool and Petey out on the lawn. "Jump in, girl. It's this or get sent back to the Humane Society."

Streak tilted her head.

"That's right," I said. "So stop fooling around. We'll make it quick."

Darci came out and pulled the hose over.

I held Petey up. "Look what Streak had. We need to give him a bath, too. I'll make sure he's okay."

Darci grinned and ran back to turn on the water.

I held the hose at arm's length. Sometimes centipedes came squirting out with the water. Nothing this time. I let water spill into the pool.

Streak watched as I gave Petey a quick bath and laid him out to dry in the sun.

"You know what, Darce? We should brush Streak's teeth, too."

We gave Streak a

double dose of dog shampoo and ran water over her head. She liked it.

"Now are we going to brush her teeth, Calvin?"

"Sure. Go get an old toothbrush. Look under the sink in our bathroom."

Darci ran into the house and I got Chewy's old toothpaste from the garage. It didn't smell all that great, but it was for dogs, right? I ran back before Streak could jump out of the swimming pool.

"Got something special for you, girl."

She smelled it.

Darci came back with a red toothbrush.

"Isn't that Stella's?" I said.

"It's her old one. It was in the bottom drawer. There weren't any under the sink."

I shrugged and squeezed out a double dose of toothpaste. "Open her mouth, Darce."

Darci wrapped her arms around Streak's muzzle and I peeled back her lips.

"This will taste good," I said. "You'll like it."

Crazy. I was brushing a dog's teeth! It was funny. Streak licked it up and smacked her lips as I worked the toothbrush around her spiky teeth. Then I got the hose and squirted water into her mouth. She barked at it.

Darci ran over and turned off the water.

"There," I said, squatting with my arms over my knees. "How can anyone complain about your breath now?"

Streak nosed me like, Hey, thanks! That was great!

When Darci came back I handed her the toothbrush. She ran inside to put it away.

Streak jumped out of the pool and shook. Already the sun was drying her black-and-white coat. I gave her a hug.

"This is the cleanest you've been since you were born, I bet."

Streak sat and scratched, her back leg working.

"And believe it or not, you smell sweet . . . sort of."

Late that afternoon when Mom got home I was sitting on the grass with Streak, trying to think of what to say in class. Was toothpaste better than mouthwash? Or maybe dogs should just stop eating fish heads and carrying around dried-up dead toads.

Mom parked in the garage and came out. She kissed the top of my head, then got down close to pet Streak. "Oh my!" She scrunched her nose.

"What?" I asked.

"Her breath smells like a peppermint swamp."

Maybe I needed stronger toothpaste.

19

Naruto

For the special occasion, Mr. Purdy brought his time-to-show-me-what-you've-got raised eyebrow to school. "All right, junior detectives, it's presentation day! You ready?"

"Yes, Mr. Purdy!" we said.

Props were everywhere. Handmade posters,

photographs, books, all kinds of objects, and two living creatures—Streak, who smelled like toothpaste, which I'd rubbed onto her teeth at the last possible minute, and Ace's parrot, BooBoo, in a cage in the back of the room. Julio had made our chart, which he was hiding until we were ready.

Mr. Purdy raised his hand. "Okay, listen up. I'm going to draw team names from my coffee cup. Whoever I draw is up."

"Bring it on!" Rubin shouted.

Mr. Purdy reached into his cup.

I crossed my fingers. Not me and Julio, please, not us first.

Mr. Purdy looked up. "Ace and Doreen!"

I sat back, relieved.

Ace got his parrot and brought it to the front of the room. He held up the cage. "Say hello, BooBoo."

"Hel-lo . . . blaaach . . . hel-lo."

The class thought that was hilarious.

Streak's ears shot straight up.

Mr. Purdy leaned back on the edge of his desk. "Tell us what your research question is, Doreen."

"Ace thought of it," she said. "He's been teaching BooBoo how to talk. He can say 'Hello,' 'Goodbye,' 'Awesome,' and 'Feed me.' So our question was this: You can teach a parrot to talk, but can you teach it to sing?"

Ace set BooBoo's cage on Mr. Purdy's desk next to the terrarium that held our class pet, Manly Stanley, a centipede. Manly slithered under his rock, probably afraid BooBoo would eat him.

BooBoo squawked.

"BooBoo," Ace said. "Sing 'Happy Birthday.'"

"*Squawk!*"

"You can do it, come on."

"*Squawk! Achh!*"

Streak barked once. I clamped a hand over her muzzle.

Ace dug into his pocket. "Here, if you sing I'll give you some Fritos."

Mr. Purdy laughed. "Your parrot likes Fritos?"

"Yeah. And sweet potato chips."

"Acch! Squaaawk!"

"'Happy birthday to you,'" Ace sang. "Come on, BooBoo, sing for us."

"Hap-py bir-day to you . . . squawk!"

Amazing! The whole class stood up and whooped and cheered and generally went bonkers until Mr. Purdy hissed, *"Sssssss."*

We settled down.

Ace gave BooBoo a piece of a Frito.

"Terrific, Ace," Mr. Purdy said. "You, too, Doreen. Did you both teach that to the bird?"

"Yeah," Ace said. "Doreen is a good teacher, too."

"Excellent."

Ace and Doreen took BooBoo to the back of the room.

Mr. Purdy reached into his coffee cup. "Who's next?"

I crossed my fingers. Not us, not us.

"Willy and Rubin!"

Rubin stood up so fast his chair fell over. He grabbed his box of props and ran up front with Willy.

Streak sat up, alert. I could imagine her thinking, This school stuff is so cool! Bring on the show!

"Start by giving us your research question, boys."

Rubin swept his hand toward the box like a magician. "In this box we have two complete sets of something I got in Japan."

He nodded to Willy. "Show them."

Willy reached in and brought out two manga books, the Japanese graphic novels you read backwards.

"Our question is: Which is better, Naruto or InuYasha?"

"Naruto!" someone called out.

"No, no, InuYasha!"

"Sssssssss," Mr. Purdy hissed. "Let them continue."

Rubin grabbed a handful of Naruto books from the box.

"Naruto stories are funny and interesting. They make you want to keep on reading. Naruto is a boy about twelve years old, and he just wants to impress people. Then there's Kakashi, who's skilled in combat. And Gaara, who has the will to kill."

Willy grabbed a few InuYashas.

"And InuYasha is about eighteen," he said.

"He's half demon and half a white-haired guy. Sometimes he's good and sometimes he's not. He wants to become a full demon by collecting shards of the Shikon Jewel. Once he gets all the shards he can piece them together and make the Jewel of Four Souls, and become a full demon."

"I see," Mr. Purdy said. "So what's your conclusion, and why?"

Rubin pinched his jaw. "Well . . . Naruto is better. He's not that smart, but he wants to be the best ninja ever . . . but InuYasha has better art."

Mr. Purdy looked at Willy. "Is that your conclusion, too, Willy?"

"To tell the truth, Mr. Purdy, I'm still trying to figure out how to read backwards."

The class roared.

I hugged Streak close. She didn't stink at all. How could Mom and Stella think she did? They just didn't want a dog, that was all.

Mom was going to make me find Streak another home. I just knew it.

I slumped in my chair as Willy and Rubin went back to their seats.

"Next up is . . . Shayla and Maya."

"Aiy," I whispered.

20

A Nose for News

The class went wild over Maya and Shayla's discovery question: "Why do boys have to smell everything? Or are they just weird?"

Ace pumped his fist and shouted, "Right on!"

All us guys stuck our noses up and started

sniffing the air. Even Mr. Purdy looked amused.

Shayla and Maya smiled and waited.

I remembered what Maya had said: *If I was you two I wouldn't even come to school on Tuesday.*

Aiy-yai-yai.

Mr. Purdy held up his hands for quiet. "Proceed, girls."

Maya and Shayla's prop was a big poster. They'd taped newspaper over it so no one could see it before they were ready. Shayla uncovered it and stood it up.

Photographs.

Of me and Julio!

Mr. Purdy bent close to look, then grinned. "This should be interesting."

I leaned over my desk and squinted at the photos.

Maya grabbed a pencil to use as a pointer. "Here we have Julio smelling his armpit."

Even I laughed at that. Streak barked, too.

"Shhhh," I said. "No barking in school."

Then I thought: Wait! How did they get that picture? It was on our street. And I was in it, too.

"I wasn't smelling my armpit," Julio shouted. "I was scratching my nose with my arm!"

Shayla went on. "And here we have Julio and Calvin scooping up dog poop with a shovel, then smelling their hands."

"Yeah, but you stepped in it," Julio called from the back row.

"I don't know what you're talking about," Shayla said.

"Oh yes you do. You were hiding down by Calvin's house. You were sneaking through the bushes where he throws all the—"

"And look at this picture," Maya interrupted. "Calvin is kissing his dog."

The class cracked up.

"No I wasn't, I was smell— I was . . . ah, forget it."

I was stuck. Smelling Streak's breath would sound worse than kissing her.

"And here's a picture of Julio smelling his fingers after throwing a dried-up dead toad down the road."

Mr. Purdy grinned. "I remember flinging dried toads myself."

I wondered: Did he ever capture a dog fut in a jar?

Maya and Shayla went on . . . and on . . . and on. After a while I didn't care anymore. I didn't even care that I won my bag-of-shrimp bet with Julio. So what? Boys smell stuff. Big deal. And anyway Maya and Shayla didn't know that all that smelling was part of our research. When we told our story, we would take theirs apart.

"Well," Mr. Purdy said. "You girls sure have a nose for news. So what's your conclusion?"

Maya glanced over at me, then back at Julio. "We decided that boys are just weird, that's all. It's not their fault. They can't help it. Good, bad, or disgusting, they gotta smell it."

Rubin jumped up. "Stinks forever!"

Mr. Purdy raised an eyebrow toward Maya and Shayla. "Does the weirdness of boys include your teacher, girls?"

"Oh, no, Mr. Purdy, not you!" Shayla looked shocked.

He chuckled. "I appreciate that. But you forgot the good stuff we boys like to smell. Our favorites are popcorn at the movies and teriyaki meat sticks at the beach, right, boys?"

We all jumped up, making smirky faces at the girls.

Mrs. Leandro from the class next door appeared in the door with her you-are-disturbing-my-class teacher look.

Mr. Purdy nodded at her, grinning. "Okay, class, pipe down. Back to work."

Mrs. Leandro vanished, and Mr. Purdy went over and shut the door.

"Who's next?" He pulled out another slip of paper, looked up, and winked.

At me.

21

A Good Stink II

I set Streak on the floor.

Julio and I stood up.

Maya and Shayla had just walked all over us. We'd have to say something pretty good to put ourselves back together again.

"Come on, girl," I whispered to Streak as Julio got our chart from the back of the room.

Streak followed me to the front. Mr. Purdy squatted down to pet her. She licked his hand.

"And what's your name?" he said.

"Streak," I said. "You can pick her up if you want."

Mr. Purdy lifted Streak up and showed her to the class.

"This is the dog I wrote about in my essay," I said.

"Ah, the one with the short attention span."

Doreen leaned over her desk. "Is that the dog you were kissing, Calvin?"

I ignored her.

Mr. Purdy sat on the table and set Streak in his lap. "Okay, boys. What did you research?"

"Stinks," Julio said. "Lots of stinks."

"See?" Maya said, jumping up. "We told you they were smelling stuff."

"Yeah, but you don't know why," Julio said.

"Sure I do. You can't help it."

Mr. Purdy hushed us. "Tell us your discovery question, boys."

Julio looked at me.

I nodded. "Okay, this is it: Why do dogs have terrible breath and what can you do about it?"

"I love it!" Mr. Purdy said. "Tell me, because I know lots of people who would like to know."

Julio gave Shayla and our traitor-friend Maya a superior look because we had Mr. Purdy on our side. "We were *smelling* things," Julio said, "because we wanted to grade stuff, bad to worse, see? Because some stinks are more worse than other stinks."

"Just worse, Julio," Mr. Purdy corrected. "Not more worse."

"Yeah, sure, Mr. Purdy. But anyway, let's start with the least worse, and that one is the stink that's only in your mind."

Huh? We didn't talk about that one. I waited for more.

Mr. Purdy, still petting Streak, cocked his head. "Tell us about that one, Julio."

Julio grinned. "Well . . . you know what? I think Rubin can explain it better than me."

The jar!

Rubin shut his eyes to make it look like he was sleeping at his desk.

"Somebody wake him up," Mr. Purdy said. "We don't want him to miss anything."

Doreen reached over and slammed Rubin's desk.

Rubin jumped and sputtered. "Uh . . . what? Huh?"

Julio was pumped now. "Okay, the best stinks are, like, when you pet a dog and smell your hand after? That's not too bad. But then you got your heavy-duty stinks, like the boys' bathroom, fresh dog doo, and dead stuff, like toads."

"And a toilet hole," I added.

Mr. Purdy tilted his head. "Toilet hole?"

"You know, the part under the toilet."

"The sewer pipe?"

"Yeah, that."

Julio shook his head. "Hoo, man! That was uku nasty!"

Half the girls were making faces. Some were covering their ears. They not only didn't want to smell bad stuff, they didn't even want to *hear* about it.

"Look," I said, holding up the chart. "We put stinks in order, the worst at the top. First the absolute worst: the toilet hole—that's the sewer pipe. Then dog doo, dead toad, dog fut—"

The class burst out laughing over that one.

I went on. "Then after that you got dog breath, cat breath, pig breath, and possibly white rat breath."

Julio felt the tip of his nose when I said that one.

Mr. Purdy looked at the poster, thinking. "Why did you come up with this question, boys?"

Julio hooked a thumb toward Streak. "Because of that dog."

STINKS
1. Toilet hole
2. Dog doo
3. Dead toad
4. Dog fut
5. Dog breath
6. Cat breath
7. Pig breath
8. White rat breath

I nodded. "Yeah, my mom and Stella—she lives with us—well, they say Streak stinks, and they don't want her in the house because of it, and . . . I wanted to think of a way to, you know . . . clean her up."

"So he can keep the dog," Julio added. "He might lose it."

"Eh?" Mr. Purdy said. "Why?"

I shrugged. "Because she stinks."

Mr. Purdy sniffed Streak. "Just smells like a dog to me."

"It's more about . . . her breath."

"Smell the dog's breath, Mr. Purdy!" Ace shouted.

Mr. Purdy grinned. "You know what, Calvin? I think the class should get involved with this. Who wants to come up and see if this dog has bad breath?"

"Eeew!"

"Not me!"

"Sick."

"It's not bad," I said. "I kind of, uh . . . brushed her teeth before school."

"Aw, man!"

"Any takers?" Mr. Purdy asked.

Nobody.

"Well," Mr. Purdy said. "I guess we'll never know."

I looked at Streak. Her tongue was jiggling in the hot classroom.

"I'll do it, Calvin." Shayla pushed her chair back and stood.

"That's brave of you, Shayla," Mr. Purdy said. "And I'm sure these boys will appreciate your courage."

Shayla came forward. She glanced at me and smiled.

I half-smiled back. "Uh . . . thanks."

"No problem, Calvin."

Mr. Purdy tucked Streak under his arm.

Everyone lurched forward to see if Shayla would gag and throw up, or something.

She leaned close to Streak and sniffed.

Streak licked her nose.

Shayla didn't even wipe it off.

Mr. Purdy raised his eyebrows. "Well?"

"It's not great, Mr. Purdy. But it is a little minty. That must be the toothpaste. It also smells like fish."

I had to agree, there was that.

"But you know what?" Shayla went on. "Most dogs have bad breath. But it's not a bad stink, it's a good stink."

That's what I said! *Exactly* what I said!

I looked at Shayla.

Mr. Purdy turned to me. "But your mom and the girl who lives with you don't quite see it that way, is that right, Calvin?"

"Pretty much."

Mr. Purdy rubbed his hand over Streak's head. "Some people are dog people, and some aren't."

"Do you have a dog, Mr. Purdy?" Julio asked.

"Sure do."

I looked at Mr. Purdy. "Does his breath stink?"

"Sometimes."

Just before the bell rang for recess, Mr. Purdy announced the winner of the detective research project. And it wasn't a team; it was a person.

Shayla.

Everyone clapped.

But no one was louder than me.

22

The Secret

Later that day, just before dinner, I was in my room when Ledward drove up.

Streak ran out of the garage to greet him.

He tossed her the silvery-blue tail of an aku. "There you go!"

Streak snapped it in midair and took it out into the yard.

That's the problem, I thought, watching through my window. That and dried-up toads.

I went outside.

"Howzit?" Ledward said, clamping a big hand down on my shoulder.

"Good."

He kept his hand on my shoulder and turned to study Streak, now ripping away at the aku tail. "I call that fish jerky for dogs. Good for their teeth and gums."

I nodded. "But it stinks up her breath."

"Like when people eat garlic for their health."

"What's garlic?"

"Smelly stuff that's good for you."

"Do you eat it?"

He laughed. "If I did your mama wouldn't let me in your house."

"Really?"

He nodded. "Maybe not even on the street to your house."

"Uh, Ledward? Do you think you could, you know, maybe bring Streak something to eat that . . . um . . . doesn't stink?"

"Hmmm." He thought, and then his eyes brightened. "Corn! I got way too much in my garden. Next time I'll bring her couple ears to chew on, how's that?"

"Sounds good to me."

Ledward grinned and gave my shoulder a squeeze. "Let's go inside. Your mama said she was cooking shepherd's pie tonight."

The kitchen smelled like heaven.

Mom was at the stove steaming broccoli. The shepherd's pie was cooling on the counter. Stella was making a salad while Darci set the table.

Ledward gave Mom a hug from behind. "Looks good."

"You hungry?"

"Like a horse."

I grabbed Streak's bowl and reached under the kitchen counter for the bag of dog food.

"I fed her earlier, honey," Mom said.

"You did?"

"She was begging."

"Oh."

"She smells better. Did you bathe her?"

"Uh, yeah . . . in Darci's pool."

"In her *swimming* pool?"

"We rinsed it out."

Mom shook her head. "Well, Streak smells better . . . though her breath is still fishy."

I glanced at Ledward.

He made an *oops* face.

Then I remembered what Shayla had said. "It's a good stink, Mom. Not a bad stink."

Mom coughed a laugh. "Well, I never thought of it quite like that before. But it does make sense. If you love your dog you don't care, right?"

That threw me. "You mean . . . you mean I can keep Streak?"

Mom cocked her head. "Why on earth would you ask that?"

"Well, because of her breath, and how you

always wash your hands after you pet her, and how you complain when she's in the house that—"

"Whoa, slow down there, Cal." Mom leaned over and looked me in the eye. "Is that what you've been thinking? That I'm going to make you give her up because she *smells*?"

"Uh . . . well . . . yeah."

Mom cupped the sides of my face with her hands. "I would never, ever make you give up your dog, Calvin. Never."

"You wouldn't?"

"Of course not. Do you think I'm heartless?"

I opened my mouth, but nothing came out.

"I love Streak as much as you do, honey."

Now I was really confused.

I looked at Stella. She puckered her lips into a fat smooch.

Mom kissed the top of my head. "Keep giving her baths. It helps."

After dinner, Darci and I watched TV.

Darci had Petey propped up to watch, too, so I guess there were three of us.

Mom and Ledward had gone out onto the dark patio to talk. The bathroom door was open, and I could see Stella washing her face.

I was thinking about how I'd gotten so worried about something that wasn't even *real* . . . when I noticed something . . . and nearly choked!

"Darce." I grabbed her arm. "Look."

Our mouths hung open, because now Stella was brushing her teeth . . . with the same red toothbrush we'd used that one time on *Streak*. She took the brush out and looked at it, moving her tongue around like something tasted bad.

Ooops.

"I thought you said it was her old one," I whispered.

"Well, it was in the bottom drawer where the old stuff is."

When Stella saw us gawking at her she kicked the door shut.

Me and Darci looked at each other, then raced outside, bursting into laughter. We stumbled into the weeds across the street, out of range. If Stella heard us she'd make us tell her what we were laughing at.

And then she'd kill us.

Streak trotted out of the garage like, What's

going on? She grabbed up a sun-dried toad on the street and brought it with her. I struggled it out of her mouth and flung it into the bushes. "Don't *chew* on those!"

Streak looked into the bushes where it had gone, her ears standing up.

I couldn't stop giggling. "Don't ever tell Stella, Darce, okay? Never, ever, ever."

"Tell who what?"

"Stella. The toothbrush."

Darci looked at me with a straight face. "What toothbrush?"

"What she doesn't know won't hurt her, right?"

"Yeah," Darci said. "But it might make her sick."

I grinned and looked back toward the house. "Calvin?"

"What?"

"You got any money?"

"Some. Why?"

"We got to buy her a new toothbrush."

I turned back. "Why?"

Darci looked up at me.

"Okay, okay," I said. "We'll get her a new one. Tomorrow. We'll sneak it in."

"Red."

"Yeah, yeah." I smiled to myself. It served Stella right for complaining about Streak.

But Darci was right. We'd get her a new one.

"You know what, Darci?"

"What?"

"You're nicer than me."

"I am?"

"Yeah . . . because I would buy her a pink one."

"Stella hates pink."

"Exactly."

Just as we were about to head back to the house, Streak ran out of the bushes and sat at my feet, the dried-up toad in her mouth.

I squatted down and looked her in the eye. "You are incurable, you know that? Absolutely one hundred percent incurable."

Streak dropped the toad.

"She wants you to have it," Darci said, squatting down to pet her. "I wish I had a dog that loved me that much."